MAHIRAVANA

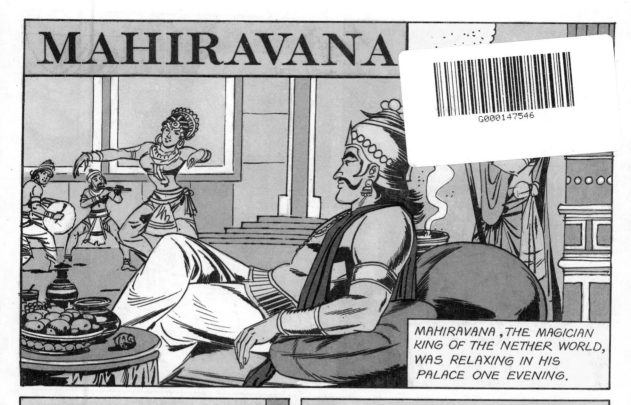

MAHIRAVANA, THE MAGICIAN KING OF THE NETHER WORLD, WAS RELAXING IN HIS PALACE ONE EVENING.

SUDDENLY, THROUGH HIS SUPERNATURAL POWERS, HE PERCEIVED THAT SOMEONE WAS IN DANGER AND NEEDED HIS HELP.

BUT WHO? WHO IS THINKING OF ME? I MUST FIND OUT.

RETIRING TO HIS CHAMBER, HE TRIED TO FIGURE OUT WHO IT WAS.

NO ONE HERE IN THE NETHER WORLD NEEDS MY HELP.

NO ONE NEEDS ME IN HEAVEN, EITHER.

HE THEN THOUGHT OF HIS KITH AND KIN LIVING ON EARTH. THEN—

AH! IT'S MY FATHER! HE IS IN DANGER! I MUST GO TO HIM IMMEDIATELY.

AS HE CHANTED A MAGIC SPELL, THE ROOF OPENED TO GIVE HIM A PATH UPWARDS TOWARDS THE EARTH.

GLIDING OUT, MAHIRAVANA STARTED FOR LANKA, WHERE HIS FATHER, RAVANA, REIGNED.

I WONDER WHAT HAS HAPPENED! FATHER HAS MANY POWERFUL RELATIVES AND GENERALS TO HELP HIM. AND YET HE SUMMONS ME....

SOON HE ARRIVED AT LANKA.

IS IT TOO LATE? THE PLACE LOOKS DESERTED. WHAT COULD HAVE HAPPENED?

MEANWHILE, RAVANA WAITED IMPATIENTLY IN HIS PALACE FOR MAHIRAVANA.

WHY IS HE TAKING SO LONG?

JUST THEN—

FATHER!

YOU HAVE COME, MY SON! I KNEW YOU WOULD NOT FAIL ME.

I AM RELIEVED TO SEE YOU, FOR I AM IN TROUBLE.

I AM THREATENED BY AN ENEMY WHO HAS ALREADY KILLED KUMBHAKARNA, INDRAJIT AND MANY OTHER MIGHTY WARRIORS.

KUMBHAKARNA AND INDRAJIT! HOW DID IT HAPPEN, FATHER? WHO IS THIS ENEMY WHO IS SO POWERFUL?

LISTEN, SON, AND I WILL TELL YOU THE WHOLE STORY.

MY SISTER WAS INSULTED BY PRINCE RAMA. TO AVENGE THE INSULT, I KIDNAPPED HIS WIFE, SITA.

THEN RAMA SENT HANUMAN, A MONKEY, IN SEARCH OF SITA. HE CAME TO LANKA AND DESTROYED MY PRECIOUS ASHOKA GROVE.

I MANAGED TO HAVE HIM BOUND AND ORDERED HIS TAIL TO BE SET ON FIRE.

4

THE WRETCHED MONKEY JUMPED FROM ROOF TO ROOF AND VERY SOON MY CITY WAS ABLAZE.

THEN RAMA CAME WITH HIS MONKEY ARMY.

HE KILLED MANY OF MY BRAVE GENERALS AND WARRIORS.

AND THAT IS WHY I NOW NEED YOUR HELP.

I CAN'T BELIEVE IT! YOU, WHO HAVE DEFEATED INDRA AND OTHER DEVAS, HAVE BEEN DEFEATED BY A BANISHED PRINCE AND A MONKEY-KING!

THEY ARE NOT ORDINARY HUMAN BEINGS, SON! THEIR VALOUR IS GREATER THAN THAT OF EVEN THE DEVAS.

OH, IF ONLY YOU HAD CALLED ME EARLIER! ALL OUR KINSMEN AND FRIENDS WOULD HAVE BEEN SAVED!

BUT, EVEN NOW, YOU CAN HELP US TO VANQUISH THE ENEMY, SON.

AND THEY STARTED MAKING PLANS.

MEANWHILE, IN RAMA'S CAMP, VIBHEESHANA* WAS ANXIOUS TO KNOW WHAT RAVANA'S NEXT MOVE WOULD BE.

MY LORD, ALL RAVANA'S MEN HAVE BEEN KILLED IN BATTLE. MAY I GO AND FIND OUT WHAT HE PLANS TO DO NEXT?

OF COURSE, VIBHEESHANA, IF YOU THINK IT IS NECESSARY.

6

*RAVANA'S BROTHER WHO HAD JOINED THE OPPOSITE CAMP

VIBHEESHANA ASSUMED THE FORM OF A BIRD AND FLEW OFF...

...TILL HE CAME TO RAVANA'S PALACE.

SO, THIS IS IT—RAVANA HAS SUMMONED MAHIRAVANA!

HE HURRIED BACK—

RAMA MUST BE INFORMED OF THIS!

REGAINING HIS NORMAL FORM, HE WENT TO RAMA.

O RAMA! RAVANA HAS SUMMONED MAHIRAVANA, WHO IS BRAVE AND SKILFUL BUT...

BUT WHAT? GO ON, VIBHEESHANA.

... IT'S HIS MAGICAL POWERS WHICH ARE TO BE FEARED MOST. HE IS A WILY PERSON. ONE CANNOT FORETELL HIS PLANS.

I SEE.....

WE MUST BE VERY CAREFUL. TONIGHT SPECIALLY WE MUST BE ALERT AND VIGILANT.

WE WILL KEEP AWAKE AND FOIL MAHIRAVANA IF HE TRIES TO PLAY ANY OF HIS TRICKS.

BUT WE MUST ALSO THINK OF A WAY OF KEEPING RAMA AND LAKSHMANA SAFE TONIGHT.

HANUMAN WAS DEEP IN THOUGHT. THEN—

YES! I HAVE IT! I'LL BUILD A STRONG FORTRESS AROUND RAMA AND LAKSHMANA SO THAT NO ONE WILL BE ABLE TO GET IN.

A FORTRESS? IN SUCH A SHORT TIME?

YES. YOU JUST WATCH!

BUT BEFORE I BEGIN, LORD RAMA, I HAVE A REQUEST TO MAKE. SET THE POWERFUL DISCUS, SUDARSHAN, ON GUARD AT THE TOP OF THE FORTRESS.

AS YOU WISH HANUMAN.

AND THEN, HANUMAN STARTED EXTENDING HIS TAIL. IT STOOD STIFF AND WENT HIGHER AND HIGHER...

...TILL IT REACHED THE SKY. IT BECAME A HUNDRED YOJANAS* LONG. THEN HE TURNED TO SUGREEVA, THE KING OF THE MONKEYS.

O KING, PLEASE SIT THERE AND HOLD RAMA ON YOUR LAP.

ANGADA WILL LIKEWISE PROTECT YOU, LAKSHMANA.

RAMA SAT ON SUGREEVA'S LAP AND LAKSHMANA SAT ON ANGADA'S LAP.

NOW OUR ENTIRE ARMY WILL POSITION ITSELF IN A CIRCLE AROUND THEM.

WE'LL DO THAT.

*ONE YOJANA = 13 KILOMETRES

9

THEN HANUMAN STARTED MAKING THE FORTRESS.

IT WAS COMPLETED SOON. THE DISCUS, SUDARSHAN, GUARDED THE SUMMIT.

VIBHEESHANA, YOU WILL KEEP GUARD ALL AROUND THE FORTRESS AND I'LL WATCH THE ENTRANCE. WE ARE NOW FULLY PREPARED FOR MAHIRAVANA.

YOU ARE RIGHT, HANUMAN. STILL...

...WE MUST BE VERY, VERY CAREFUL. THAT MAGICIAN CAN ASSUME ANY GUISE. SO PLEASE DON'T LET ANYONE ENTER THE FORTRESS — NOT EVEN YOUR OWN FATHER, PAWAN.*

DON'T WORRY, VIBHEESHANA, I WON'T. NO ONE WILL BE ALLOWED TO GET IN.

WHEN NIGHT FELL, THEY CONTINUED THEIR VIGIL.

* THE WIND GOD

11

MEANWHILE, IN LANKA, RAVANA AND MAHIRAVANA WERE NOT IDLE. THEY, TOO, WERE MAKING CAREFUL PLANS.

NOW FATHER, LEAVE EVERYTHING TO ME. I'LL TAKE RAMA AND LAKSHMANA AWAY TO THE NETHER WORLD AND SACRIFICE THEM THERE TO THE GODDESS, DURGA.

YOU HAVE TAKEN A LOAD OFF MY CHEST, SON.

MAHIRAVANA DEPARTED. HE TOOK NO MEN, NO HORSES AND NO WEAPONS. ENDOWED AS HE WAS WITH MAGIC POWERS, WITHIN MINUTES HE HAD REACHED RAMA'S CAMP.

HMM...VERY CLEVER! THE DISCUS BARS THE WAY FROM THE SKY.

RAMA AND LAKSHMANA MUST BE IN THAT FORTRESS. BUT HOW SHALL I GET PAST THE MONKEY TO REACH THEM?

THAT WAS INDEED A DIFFICULT PROBLEM, FOR HANUMAN WAS KEEPING A STRICT WATCH.

I WILL KEEP GUARD ROUND THE FORTRESS. REMEMBER, NOT EVEN YOUR FATHER IS TO BE ALLOWED IN.

BUT SOON AFTER VIBHEESHANA LEFT—

O MIGHTY HANUMAN! I AM DASHARATHA, RAMA'S FATHER. LET ME ENTER. I WANT TO MEET MY SONS.

KING DASHARATHA!

PLEASE WAIT FOR A MINUTE, MY LORD. VIBHEESHANA WILL SOON BE COMING THIS WAY AND WILL TAKE YOU IN.

AH! HERE HE COMES.

KING DASHARATHA IS HERE, VIBHEESHANA, TO MEET HIS SONS.

KING DASHARATHA? I SEE NO ONE HERE!

HERE.... OH! BUT WHERE HAS HE GONE?

IT MUST HAVE BEEN MAHIRAVANA IN DISGUISE! BE CAREFUL NOW. REMEMBER, YOU ARE NOT TO LET ANYONE ENTER.

HE WON'T FOOL ME AGAIN, O NOBLE ONE!

AS SOON AS VIBHEESHANA LEFT ON HIS ROUNDS—

O HANUMAN, I HAVE NOT SEEN MY BROTHERS FOR A VERY LONG TIME! PLEASE LET ME GO IN.

PRINCE BHARATA! YOUR BROTHERS WILL BE HAPPY TO MEET YOU. BUT PLEASE WAIT FOR VIBHEESHANA.

BUT WHEN VIBHEESHANA CAME THERE—

HERE COMES VIBHEESHANA. HE'LL ESCORT YOU....

TO WHOM ARE YOU TALKING? THERE'S NO ONE HERE!

THE NEXT MOMENT—

VIBHEESHANA, WHEN DID YOU COME OUT? I DIDN'T SEE YOU COMING OUT.

COMING OUT FROM WHERE, MY FRIEND? I HAVE BEEN OUT ALL THE TIME.

B...BUT...YOU WENT IN JUST NOW—TO TIE PROTECTIVE STRINGS ON THE WRISTS OF RAMA AND LAKSHMANA. OR, ARE YOU....

WHAT ARE YOU TALKING ABOUT? I DIDN'T GO IN AT ALL!

YOU ARE LYING! YOU ARE A SPY OF RAVANA, I AM SURE! YOU PLAYED THIS TRICK UPON US...YOU...!

CALM DOWN, HANUMAN. IT SEEMS THE CLEVER MAHIRAVANA HAS TRICKED YOU BY COMING IN MY GUISE THIS TIME.

YOU COULD BE RIGHT! LET'S GO IN AND SEE.

FEAR GRIPPED THEM BOTH. THEY RUSHED INSIDE.

LOOK!

RAMA AND LAKSHMANA ARE NOT HERE!

EVERY ONE IS FAST ASLEEP. AS IF BY MAGIC....

THIS IS MAHIRAVANA'S WORK! SPRINKLING THIS MAGIC POWDER BEFORE THEM...

...HE PUT THE MIGHTY WARRIORS TO SLEEP AND CARRIED RAMA AND LAKSHMANA AWAY WITH HIM THROUGH THE TUNNEL.

ALL IS LOST! PLEASE FORGIVE ME, VIBHEESHANA, FOR SUSPECTING YOU.

DON'T WORRY ABOUT THAT, HANUMAN. LET'S WAKE THE OTHERS UP.

WAKE UP, O SUGREEVA! WAKE UP, ANGADA!

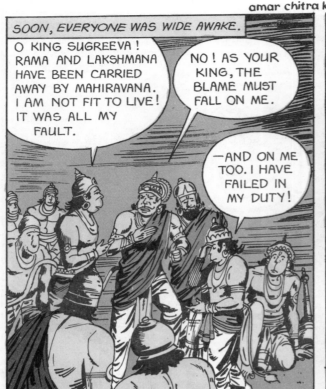

SOON, EVERYONE WAS WIDE AWAKE.

O KING SUGREEVA! RAMA AND LAKSHMANA HAVE BEEN CARRIED AWAY BY MAHIRAVANA. I AM NOT FIT TO LIVE! IT WAS ALL MY FAULT.

NO! AS YOUR KING, THE BLAME MUST FALL ON ME.

—AND ON ME TOO. I HAVE FAILED IN MY DUTY!

THEN JAMBAVAN, THE WISE ONE, SPOKE OUT.

THE BLAME MUST BE SHARED EQUALLY BY ALL OF US. BUT WHY WASTE TIME? LET US THINK OF A WAY OF RESCUING THEM. HANUMAN SHOULD GO AND FIND THEM.

YES. IF ANYONE CAN FIND THEM, IT IS HANUMAN.

O HANUMAN, YOU CROSSED THE MIGHTY OCEAN TO RESCUE SITA. ONLY YOU CAN PERFORM THIS TASK NOW. WE DEPEND UPON YOU.

MY HEAD BOWS LOW WITH SHAME, MY LORD, FOR I LET THE DEAR ONES BE CARRIED AWAY UNDER OUR VERY EYES!

TO ATONE I'LL SEARCH THE THREE WORLDS TILL I FIND THEM, FOR WITHOUT THEM I CANNOT LIVE.

HANUMAN'S TAIL CAME BACK TO ITS NORMAL SIZE. BIDDING THEM FAREWELL, HANUMAN ENTERED THE TUNNEL MADE BY MAHIRAVANA.

HE TRAVELLED THROUGH THE LONG TUNNEL...

...TILL AT LAST HE REACHED THE END.

THE NETHER WORLD STRETCHED OUT IN FRONT OF HIM.

HOW SHALL I FIND THEM IN THIS VAST PLACE?

HE SEARCHED ONE TOWN AFTER ANOTHER IN THE NETHER WORLD. AT LAST—

AH! THIS LOOKS LIKE MAHIRAVANA'S CAPITAL! I FEEL CERTAIN I'LL FIND RAMA AND LAKSHMANA HERE.

THEN HE SAW A BEAUTIFUL LAKE. ASSUMING A VERY SMALL FORM, HE WAITED ON A HIGH TREE.

I HOPE NO ONE WILL NOTICE ME.

BUT HE WAS SPOTTED BY SOME WOMEN WHO HAD COME THERE TO FETCH WATER.

LOOK! A MONKEY!

HOW TINY IT IS!

I WONDER WHERE IT HAS COME FROM!

A MONKEY HERE? THIS DOES NOT AUGUR WELL FOR OUR KING.

WHY? OUR KING FEARS NOTHING. HE IS STRONGER THAN ANYONE IN THE THREE WORLDS!

YES, BUT HE IS NOT IMMORTAL. ACCORDING TO A PROPHECY HE WILL MEET HIS END WHEN MONKEYS AND MEN COME HERE—AND HERE IS A MONKEY.

AND I HEAR THAT OUR KING HAS BROUGHT TWO MEN HERE AS HIS CAPTIVES!

TWO MEN! THEN MY LORD RAMA AND HIS BROTHER ARE HERE!

I MUST NOT WASTE ANY TIME.

JUST THEN A TERRIBLE DIN STARTLED HIM.

WHAT IS THAT NOISE? WHAT'S HAPPENING AT THE PALACE?

TELL US, OLD MOTHER, WHY ARE SO MANY PRIESTS HURRYING TOWARDS THE PALACE?

IT'S A SECRET. I CAN'T TELL YOU ABOUT IT.

NO, NO. YOU MUST TELL US!

YES, YOU MUST!

ALL RIGHT. COME CLOSER.

BUT YOU MUST NOT TELL ANYONE ELSE, OR I'LL BE IN TROUBLE!

WE WON'T TELL A SINGLE PERSON.

HANUMAN BECAME VERY ATTENTIVE.

IN A SHORT WHILE, TWO HUMAN BEINGS WILL BE SACRIFICED TO THE GODDESS DURGA.

WHO ARE THEY?

WHERE HAVE THEY COME FROM?

WHERE ARE THEY NOW?

THEY ARE THE MOST HANDSOME CREATURES I HAVE EVER SEEN! POOR SOULS! AT THE MOMENT THEY ARE LOCKED UP IN A SECRET ROOM. BUT...ENOUGH... NO MORE. OFF YOU GO... AND REMEMBER YOUR PROMISE.

WE'LL BE ABSOLUTELY SILENT, MOTHER.

HANUMAN JUMPED DOWN FROM THE TREE...

I MUST HURRY NOW.

22

...AND FOLLOWING IN THE DIRECTION OF THE NOISE, HE QUICKLY FOUND MAHIRAVANA'S PALACE.

HE SEARCHED EVERYWHERE TILL HE CAME TO A TEMPLE.

AH—THIS SEEMS TO BE THE PLACE WHERE THE SACRIFICE IS TO BE PERFORMED.

INSIDE THE TEMPLE HE FOUND A SECRET CHAMBER—

THEY ARE HERE! AT LAST I HAVE FOUND THEM!

ASSUMING THE FORM OF A FLY...

...HANUMAN FLEW INTO THE CHAMBER.

THEN HE REGAINED HIS NORMAL FORM.

WAKE UP, MY LORDS! I HAVE COME TO RESCUE YOU!

RAMA AND LAKSHMANA GOT UP WITH A START.

WHERE ARE WE?

WHAT'S HAPPENING?

YOU ARE IN THE NETHER WORLD, THE PRISONERS OF MAHIRAVANA. HE BROUGHT YOU HERE USING HIS MAGICAL POWERS.

HOW CAN WE FIGHT THESE RAKSHASAS? I DON'T EVEN HAVE MY WEAPONS WITH ME.

I'LL FIGHT THE RAKSHASAS, O RAMA. LET ME, YOUR EVER FAITHFUL SERVANT, DESTROY THIS MAGICIAN ONCE AND FOR ALL.

HANUMAN THEN TOLD THEM OF MAHIRA-VANA'S PLANS TO SACRIFICE THEM TO DURGA.

LISTEN, O RAMA. ON MY WAY HERE, I SAW GODDESS DURGA. I'LL GO AND ASK HER FOR HELP.

ALL I NEED NOW IS YOUR BLESSING, MY LORD!

YOU ARE A TRUE FRIEND, HANUMAN. MAY YOU BE SUCCESSFUL.

ONCE AGAIN ASSUMING THE FORM OF A FLY, HANUMAN FLEW TO THE GODDESS.

SALUTATIONS, O GODDESS! I AM HANUMAN, A SERVANT OF RAMA.

THE EVIL MAHIRAVANA INTENDS TO SACRIFICE RAMA AND LAKSHMANA TO YOU. TELL ME, HAS THIS BEEN ORDERED BY YOU?

NO, NO! I HAVE NOT ORDERED ANY SACRIFICE!

BUT MAHIRAVANA WORSHIPS YOU. WILL YOU HELP HIM? FOR IF YOU DO....

DON'T BE IMPATIENT, HANUMAN. LISTEN TO ME FIRST.

MAHIRAVANA WANTS TO GET RID OF HIS ENEMIES. THAT IS WHY HE IS SACRIFICING THEM. HE IS NOT DOING IT TO PLEASE ME.

SO YOU WON'T HELP HIM?

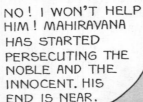

NO! I WON'T HELP HIM! MAHIRAVANA HAS STARTED PERSECUTING THE NOBLE AND THE INNOCENT. HIS END IS NEAR.

GOOD! THEN TELL ME HOW TO DESTROY HIM.

LISTEN CAREFULLY. RAMA AND LAKSHMANA WILL BE BROUGHT HERE SOON. YOU SHOULD ACCOMPANY THEM UNSEEN AND THEN....

WHEN THE GODDESS HAD FINISHED TELLING HANUMAN THE COURSE TO TAKE—

THANK YOU, O GODDESS! YOU HAVE SOLVED ALL MY PROBLEMS.

HANUMAN THEN RETURNED TO RAMA AND ASSUMED HIS OWN FORM.

THE GODDESS WAS VERY HELPFUL, MY LORD. SHE HAS SUGGESTED A CLEVER PLAN.

GOOD. TELL ME THE PLAN QUICKLY FOR THERE IS VERY LITTLE TIME LEFT.

HANUMAN TOLD RAMA WHAT WAS TO BE DONE.

SOON—

BRING THE PRISONERS OUT.

HANUMAN MADE HIMSELF INVISIBLE AND FOLLOWED RAMA AND LAKSHMANA TO THE TEMPLE.

HA...HA! IT'S THE MIGHTY RAMA! YOU WERE VERY AMBITIOUS INDEED, RAMA, TO HAVE CHALLENGED MY FATHER! TODAY YOUR LIFE IS IN MY HANDS.

SOON YOU'LL DIE AND MY FATHER WILL MARRY SITA.

THE RITUAL BEGAN—

ALMIGHTY GODDESS! I BOW TO YOU!

HAND ME THE SWORD.

AFTER PURIFYING THE SWORD, HE OFFERED IT TO THE GODDESS.

ACCEPT THIS OFFERING, O GODDESS!

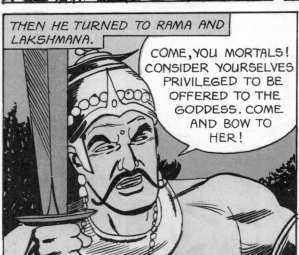

THEN HE TURNED TO RAMA AND LAKSHMANA.

COME, YOU MORTALS! CONSIDER YOURSELVES PRIVILEGED TO BE OFFERED TO THE GODDESS. COME AND BOW TO HER!

BUT THEY DIDN'T BUDGE.

MAHIRAVANA WAS ENRAGED.

WHAT? DIDN'T YOU HEAR ME? YOU DARE TO DISOBEY ME! COME FORWARD AND BOW!

WE ARE PRINCES OF AYODHYA, MAHIRAVANA. PEOPLE BOW TO US! WE HAVE NEVER BOWED TO ANY ONE IN OUR LIFE.

28

WITH TWO MORE BLOWS, HANUMAN SMASHED THE CHAINS THAT BOUND RAMA AND LAKSHMANA.

THEN HE TURNED TO DEAL WITH THE DEMONS—

COME FORWARD IF YOU WISH TO CHALLENGE ME. DO YOU DARE?

RUN!

WITHOUT MAHIRAVANA WE ARE LOST!

YOU ACTED PROMPTLY, BRAVE HANUMAN! YOU SAVED OUR LIVES TODAY.

I AM YOUR HUMBLE SERVANT AS ALWAYS, MY LORD.

SOON THEY STARTED ON THEIR JOURNEY BACK.

MEANWHILE IN SUGREEVA'S CAMP—

IT IS PAST NOON AND THEY HAVE NOT YET RETURNED. WHAT COULD HAVE HAPPENED TO THEM?

I'M SURE HANUMAN WILL NOT FAIL. LET'S TRY TO REMAIN CALM.

JUST THEN—

LOOK, KING SUGREEVA! THEY'VE COME!

MAHIRAVANA IS DEAD, FRIENDS.

AND RAVANA HAS NO ONE LEFT TO FIGHT FOR HIM!

HE'LL HAVE TO COME TO THE BATTLEFIELD HIMSELF TO FIGHT. AND THEN...

...VICTORY WILL BE OURS!

VICTORY TO RAMA!